This book belongs to

TOUGH TIMES IN TATER TOWN

A Lesson in Being Respectful

by **Bobbi JG Weiss** & **David Cody Weiss**

Illustrated by
Warner McGee

SCHOLASTIC INC.

New York Toronto London Auckland Sydney
Mexico City New Delhi Hong Kong Buenos Aires

The Pirates Who Don't Do Anything were doing what they do best—nothing! Well, they were munching on Mr. Twisty's Twisted Cheese Curls, their favorite cheesy-licious snack; but other than that, they weren't doing much.

"You know, not doing anything is making me really tired," said Larry.

Pirate Lunt yawned. "Me, too. Maybe we should try *not* doing something else for a change."

"Or we could go on a vacation!" Pa Grape suggested. "People go on vacation when they want a break from doing what they usually do."

Larry had to think about that. "But in our case, we want a break from *not* doing what we usually *don't*."

The three pirates grinned. "**Let's *do it!*"**

The pirates decided to go to Tater Town, a fancy vacation resort with a fun amusement park. They quickly set sail.

Well, okay, they didn't actually sail. They hired a tugboat to pull their pirate ship to Tater Town. Along the way, they munched cheese curls and jumped up and down a lot. Oh boy, were they excited!

Once they arrived in Tater Town, the pirates couldn't wait to visit the amusement park. They hailed Tater Tim's Tater Town Taxi to take them to the festivities.

"Hop aboard," said friendly Tater Tim.

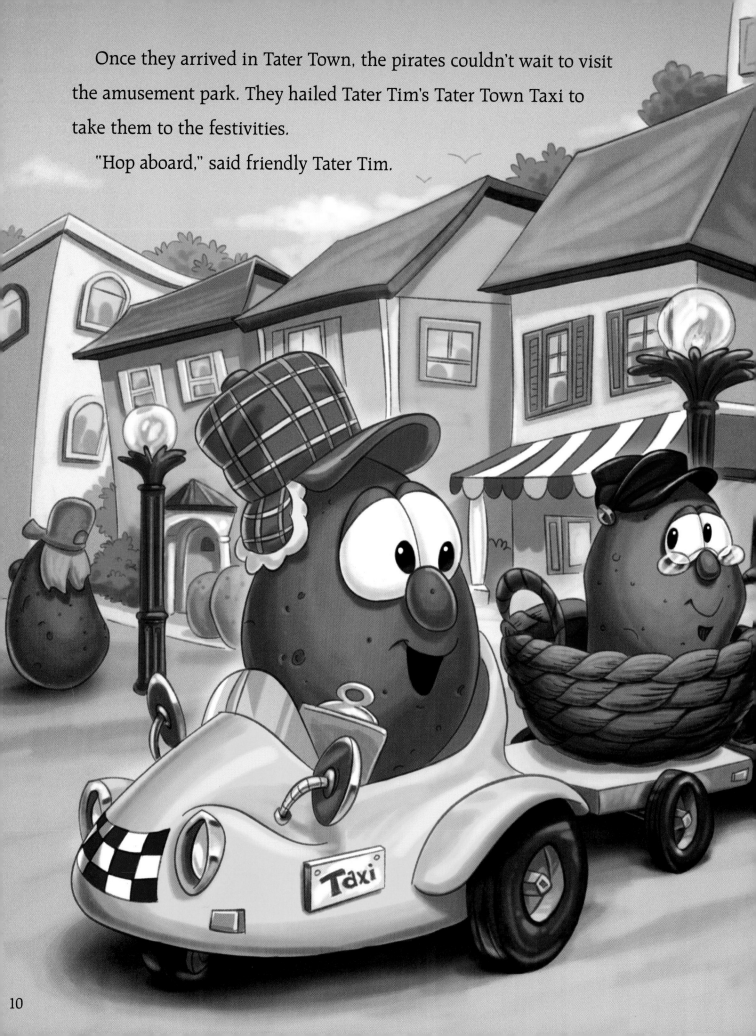

Larry stared at the strange vehicle. "This isn't a taxi," he said. "Where are the seats?"

"We don't have seats in Tater Town," said Tater Tim. "We sit in baskets."

Larry shook his head. "I can't do that. It's just plain weird."

"And it looks funny," said Pirate Lunt. "This taxi isn't like our taxis back home."

Pa Grape said to Tater Tim, "Thanks, matey, but I think we'll walk."

As the three pirates shuffled off to the amusement park, they noticed something even weirder than the Tater Town Taxi.

"Look," Larry said. "Everybody is wearing big silly hats."

Pirate Lunt saw a street vendor. "And this guy is selling big silly hats," he said.

"Distinguished guests, welcome to Tater Town! I'm Tater Ted, the Big Silly Hat Guy!" said Tater Ted. "Care to buy a big silly hat? It's tradition here in Tater Town."

The pirates looked quizzically at each other.

"Uh—I don't think so," Larry said. "They're so big."

"And silly," Pirate Lunt added.

"And I already have a hat," finished Pa Grape. "Thanks anyway."

The pirates made it to the amusement park and went in. It was wonderful! There were rides and games and clowns and balloons and food—they didn't know where to begin!

Then Larry gasped. "I don't believe it!" he cried. "They have a tic-tac-toe booth!"

Pirate Lunt hopped up and down. "Our favorite game!"

"We can pretend we're playing it on Pa Grape's hat," Larry agreed and laughed.

"My what?" Pa Grape asked suspiciously.

Grinning, Larry and Pirate Lunt said, "Never mind."

But when they reached the booth, they found out the game wasn't tic-tac-toe at all.

"Welcome!" greeted Tater Tammy. "Care to play stick-brick-blot?"

"Well, we would, but it's kind of strange," said Larry. "There are no tics."

"Or tacs," added Pirate Lunt.

"Or toes," Pa Grape finished.

"Sticks, bricks, and blots work just as well,"
said Tater Tammy. "Give it a try!"

Larry shook his head. "I don't think so. This wouldn't look right on Pa Grape's hat at all."

"Not at all," agreed Pirate Lunt.

"My what?" Pa Grape asked suspiciously.

Larry and Pirate Lunt frowned and said, "Never mind."

Time went by, but the pirates weren't having much fun. The amusement park was so odd! Larry wanted to ride the Ferris wheel, but the Taters only had a Ferris square. Pirate Lunt wanted to ride the roller coaster, but the Taters only had a bouncy coaster. And Pa Grape wanted to play the booth games, but the only prizes the Taters gave out were bananas. He wanted to win a pirate parrot plush doll.

"This place is wild," Larry complained.

"It isn't like home, that's for sure," said Pirate Lunt.

"I'll never get a pirate parrot plush doll at this rate," said Pa Grape.

The pirates needed a snack before deciding what to do. Pirate Lunt ordered three bags of Mr. Twisty's Twisted Cheese Curls.

"I'm sorry, we don't have those here," said Tater Tom. "Why don't you try the traditional Tater Town snack instead?"

Tater Tom handed Pirate Lunt and Larry a colorful snack package. "These are Mr. Linear's Not Bent Cheese Straights. They're cheesy-licious!"

"Cheese—Straights?" Pirate Larry stammered in shock.

"This is just too bizarre!"

"Look, friend," said Tater Tom. "You should show a little respect for how we do things here in Tater Town. Different isn't wrong, you know."

The Pirates Who Don't Do Anything looked at each other.

"He has a point," said Pa Grape thoughtfully.

Larry agreed. "Maybe we should give the place a chance."

The three pirates grinned and shouted, "**Let's *do it!***"

They each tried a package of Mr. Linear's Not Bent Cheese Straights.

And you know what? They loved them!

"Munchy!" munched Larry.

"Crunchy!" crunched Pa Grape.

Pirate Lunt summed it up, "They're cheesy-licious!"

The pirates decided to give big silly hats a try, too.

"How do I look?" Pa Grape asked.

"Very dashing," said Pirate Lunt.

Grinning, Pa Grape announced, "I'll buy it!"

Larry turned out to be a whiz at stick-brick-blot.

Tater Tammy happily announced, "And the winner is Pirate Larry—*again!*"

"This game is fun!" admitted Larry. "Though I still think it will look weird when we play it on Pa Grape's hat."

"My what?" Pa Grape asked suspiciously.

Larry and Pirate Lunt smiled and said, "Never mind."

At the end of the day, the pirates took Tater Tim's Tater Town Taxi back to their ship. They had a ball riding in the baskets.

"This was so much fun!" said Larry.

"Let's come back tomorrow!"

"Okay," his friends agreed.

"You know, I'm glad we decided to give Tater Town traditions a try,"
Pirate Lunt said after a while.

"Yeah," said Larry. "If we hadn't, look at all the fun we would have missed."

"Say, when we get back to the ship, let's play a game of stick-brick-blot,"
Larry said, winking at Pirate Lunt.

"Okay, and Pa Grape can take a *nap*," Pirate Lunt added slyly, winking back.
Pa Grape yawned. "Sounds good to me, mateys!"

Show proper respect to everyone . . .
1 Peter 2:17